ESCAPE
from Everytown

by Terrance Dicks

Illustrated by Chris Priestley

 LONGMAN

Contents

Chapter 1

Everytown – and Old Town

It was a lovely day in Everytown. The sun shone down at regulation strength from climate-controlled blue skies. A cool breeze swept through tree-lined avenues at carefully timed intervals. It was peaceful in the tree-shaded central plaza. The fountain played soothingly, sprinkling the surrounding trees with diamond drops.

Suddenly a dot appeared in the distance on one of the long, straight avenues radiating out from the plaza. It grew bigger and bigger and turned into a girl on a mountain bike pedalling furiously. Without slowing down, she whizzed down the little avenue that led to the square, and skidded to a halt by the fountain. In one swift movement, she swung down from the bike, leant it against the wall around the fountain and flung herself on to one of the benches that surrounded it.

People in Everytown had nice houses to live in, good food, nice clothes. They had wall-sized televisions with twenty-four hour programming, music centres, superkitchens, supermarkets, shopping malls – everything anyone could want.

There were still problems. The girl was one of the problems. She was called Kim. She had a thin sharp face, long spindly legs, fierce green eyes and hair like an explosion in a haystack.

Kim was bored, and so were most of her friends. Sometimes, when they were bored they got up to mischief. Nothing very serious – soap powder in the fountains, skateboarding in the supermarket, that sort of thing.

The law-abiding people of Everytown were horrified. "What more do these kids want?" they asked.

The trouble was, the kids didn't know themselves. But they wanted something.

Kim sat sprawled out on the bench, gazing angrily at the fountain. The fountain splashed soothingly at her. "Shut up, you!" snarled Kim.

The fountain ignored her, making calm, watery sounds.

"That's the trouble," thought Kim, "Everyone ignores you in Everytown! How can you be a rebel when they never even notice?"

She heard a distant rumbling and rattling but she didn't look up. She knew what it was.

The rattling and rumbling grew nearer and turned into a small, bespectacled boy on a skateboard. He circled the bench, spun the skateboard to a spectacular stop, and jumped off. He perched on the other end of the bench, elbows on bony knees, chin in hands. He didn't speak. Arnie never said much.

Sam, the third arrival, was broad and stocky with cropped hair, a bright blue tracksuit and huge roller-skates. He flew down the avenue, feet scarcely touching the ground, sped across the plaza, and hurdled the back of the bench – landing neatly between Arnie and Kim.

For a moment or two the three friends sat staring into the little pond that surrounded the fountain.

"Saturday again," said Kim at last.

"Then Sunday," said Sam.

"Followed," added Arnie helpfully, "by Monday – and school."

"I hate school," said Kim. She didn't really – not all the time. But in her present mood she hated everything.

"Yes but at least there's something to hate," said Sam. "Staff, lessons, other kids ... Weekends there's just nothing."

"Mum wants me to go shopping with her," said Kim. "I hate shopping! Shopping malls make me sick!"

Sam nodded. "Dad wants me to help him clean the car. When we've cleaned it, we're all going for a nice drive in the country. That'll get the car dirty so we can clean it again on Sunday."

"My lot want me to come for a nice healthy walk in the park," said Arnie. "I'm the indoor type. I hate healthy walks – especially in the park."

"Stay in and play with your old computer then," suggested Kim.

Arnie shook his head. "I defeated the Dragon Guards, reached the Sacred Altar of the Temple of Horror and zapped Bongo the Unspeakable three times yesterday. What's the point?

All three stared into the blank hours ahead.

"Well," said Kim at last. "We've got to do something."

"That's the whole point," said Sam. "There's nothing to do in this dump!"

"We could go over to Old Town," said Kim.

"Oh, sure!" said Arnie mockingly.

Old Town was across the river. It had been there since before Everytown was built. It had been left standing as a horrible example of what things were like in the Bad Old Days. Once Everytown had been built, with everything bright and clean and modern, everyone left Old Town. Nearly everyone ... There were strange rumours about Old Town.

"Why not?" said Sam suddenly. "Why shouldn't we take a look at Old Town?

"Well, no one ever goes there," said Arnie feebly. "I mean, nobody ever wants to ..."

Kim stood up. "Well, I want to!"

"It'd be something different," said Sam. "An adventure."

"That's right," said Kim. "An adventure – and not on a computer screen either." She swung a leg over her bike. "Coming?"

Sam jumped up. "You're on! Arnie?"

"Oh well," said Arnie. "I suppose so ..." Slowly he got up and moved towards his skateboard.

Minutes later three figures were speeding towards the bridge that led to Old Town. Kim led the way, tangled hair streaming out behind her. Sam skated along close behind, skimming easily over the ground. Arnie trundled along a reluctant third.

The old stone bridge rose up before them, spanning the broad, slow-moving river in a gentle arc. Kim pedalled to the middle and paused, waiting for the others to catch up. Behind them lay the neatly planned streets and parks and avenues of Everytown, with its bright, pastel-coloured buildings. Ahead were the dark and twisted streets of Old Town.

"Well, here goes," said Kim, and pushed off down the slope. Sam followed, then Arnie.

One by one the streets of Old Town swallowed them up.

Everything seemed different in Old Town.

It was cooler for a start. The sky was grey, not blue and the sun broke fitfully through the clouds.

The streets were different too. The streets of Old Town didn't run in neat, sensible lines. Instead they wandered crazily in all directions. Grimy buildings of every shape and size, decorated with towers and turrets and odd-shaped windows, seemed to lean menacingly over the narrow streets. Old Town was *unplanned.*

There was a sudden, brief shower of rain. Arnie looked astonished. "It isn't due to rain till twelve o'clock."

In Everytown it only rained at mealtimes, when everyone was inside.

"I think it rains when it wants to here," said Sam.

They tried to imagine weather that kept changing, rather than sun and rain at the regular times.

The rain stopped as suddenly as it had begun. "Weird!" said Kim. She was cycling as slowly as she could, and the others kept pace. Old Town didn't seem to be a place to rush into.

Then they saw the café. It was on the corner of a little square, a ramshackle-looking place with metal tables and chairs out on the pavement.

They stopped to look at it and a fat, cheerful-looking man in an apron came out and nodded to them. "What can I get you? Tea? Coffee? Lemonade?"

Kim looked at the others. "Lemonade?" They all nodded and Kim said, "Lemonade please."

The man went into the café. Kim leaned her bike against the wall, Arnie parked his skateboard and Sam took off his skates. They sat down at one of the tables.

The man reappeared with a tin tray holding three fizzing glasses. He put the tray down on the table and watched as Kim picked up her glass and drank. "It tastes of lemons!" she said.

The café man smiled. "What else? Visiting from Everytown?"

"How did you know?"

"Not many kids left in Old Town now. We get a few over from Everytown from time to time. Looking for something?"

Kim nodded. "I suppose so – but I'm not sure what it is. Do you know?"

"I might," said the café man.

"What do the people who live here do?" asked Arnie.

The man laughed. "Do? They live! They work, they shop, they stroll, they chat. Look!"

He waved his hand and they saw that the little square had suddenly become busy. Shops had opened and people were going from one to another, buying something here, something there. They were stopping to say good morning, chatting with one another outside shops and on street corners.

"Those shops are all selling different things," said Kim suddenly. "Meat in one, fish in another, vegetables in another. It could take you all morning to shop. We whizz round the hypermarket in an hour!"

"Ah, but do you enjoy it?" said the café man. "Do you chat to the shopkeeper, find out all the local news and gossip?"

"What do you do for entertainment in Old Town?" said Sam. "Have you got round-the-clock satellite supertelly like us?"

"And video games?" asked Arnie.

The man shook his head. "There's a theatre and a

cinema. Otherwise, we walk, we talk – and there's reading, of course."

"Reading?" repeated Kim in amazement.

"That's right. You can still read in Everytown, can't you?"

"Of course we can," said Arnie indignantly. "We do lots of reading. The lessons on our computer screens at school, public notices on television, video game instructions ... "

"What about books?" asked the café man.

Sam stared at him. "You mean those square things made from sheets of paper stuck together all down one side?"

"I saw one once in a museum," said Kim.

The man nodded. "That's right, books. I like a good thriller myself." He produced a square object from his apron pocket. It had a bright yellow cover with words in black lettering: *The Four Just Men* by Edgar Wallace.

"What do you do with it?" asked Kim.

"You sit down and you read it, page by page." The café man handed Kim the book. Suddenly she was looking at the body of a distinguished, middle-aged man slumped over his desk, a telephone on his hand. She rubbed her eyes and hurriedly passed the book back. "Where did you get it?"

"From the Library, of course."

Kim finished her lemonade and stood up. "You said you might know what we were looking for?"

"Magic," said the man. "It's all been planned out of Everytown but there's quite a bit left over here."

"Have they got any at this library?"

"Stacks of it!"

"How do you get there?"

"Across the square, down that street and then straight up the hill. You can't miss it."

Kim looked at the others. "Coming, you lot?"

Arnie got his skateboard and Sam his skates.

"How much for the lemonade?" asked Kim.

"My treat," said the café man. "Special offer for first-time customers. Come back and let me know how you got on – if you can. Oh, and watch out for the Guardian!"

"What Guardian?"

Some more customers arrived at one of the tables and the man went off to serve them. Kim and Sam and Arnie set off across the square.

"I wonder what he meant by watch out for the Guardian?" said Sam.

"Only one way to find out," said Kim.

They set off to find the Library.

Chapter 2

The Guardian

"Well," said Kim. "There it is!"

Arnie looked up at the grim building towering above them. "All right, we found it," he said. "Let's go home!"

Kim understood how he felt. There was something pretty scary about the Library. A huge, gloomy-looking building, it towered over the winding streets of Old Town like a castle on a hill. A long flight of steps led up to a massive metal door, flanked by great stone pillars.

Kim looked at Sam. "What do you think?"

Sam shrugged. "Might as well take a look inside – now we've come this far."

Kim got off her bike and started to wheel it up the steps. Sam took off his skates, tucked them under his arm and followed. Arnie picked up his skateboard and trailed after them.

They all gathered outside the big door. It was a double door made from some dull green metal and covered with ornamental scroll work. In its centre were two massive round handles worn shiny with age. Kim pushed the right-hand one. It didn't move.

"They're closed," said Arnie happily. "Come on, let's go!"

Kim pushed at the other handle and the left-hand door swung silently open. She went inside and found herself in a gloomy, marble-floored entrance hall lit by shafts of light from stained-glass windows set high in the wall. To the left a curved flight of stairs led upwards into the gloom. Directly ahead on the far side of the hall was a long counter made of darkly gleaming wood.

Sam followed her through the door and then Arnie.

"There's no one here," said Sam. Arnie let go of the door and it closed with a crash that echoed around the hall.

"Close the door *quietly!*" boomed a voice from across the hall. A tall shape had appeared behind the counter. "You may leave your transportation by the door," the voice

went on. "This is a library, not a garage or a garden shed. Put those objects down and *come here!*"

It was the sort of voice you didn't even think about disobeying. Leaving bike, skates and skateboard, they crossed the hall and stood before the counter, looking up at the extraordinary figure on the other side – an incredibly tall woman in a long dress made from shiny black material. She wore long, dangly black earrings and a necklace of black beads. Her grey hair was piled amazingly high on her head. She had a long white face, a beaky nose upon which perched gold-rimmed glasses and long white hands.

"She looks really strange," thought Kim.

"I am the Guardian," announced the woman as if that explained everything. "Hands!"

Kim stared at her. "I'm sorry?"

"Show me your hands so I can see if they're clean."

"Bossy-boots!" thought Kim, but she held out her hands just the same. So did the others.

The Guardian sniffed. "I suppose they'll do. Names!"

"Look," said Sam, "we haven't come to join or anything."

"We just wanted a quick look round," said Arnie.

"What's the matter?" snapped the Guardian. "Afraid of books?"

Her tone stung Arnie into defiance. "Afraid? No, of course not."

"Why should anyone be afraid of books?" asked Sam.

The Guardian smiled grimly. "Very well. Then join. Names!" She pointed a long bony finger at Kim. "You first!"

Kim opened her mouth to argue, then closed it again. "Best thing to do is to humour her," she thought.

One by one they gave their names and addresses. The Guardian wrote them all down in a big leather-covered book, using a steel-nibbed, wooden pen dipped into a metal inkwell.

"Haven't you got a computer?" asked Arnie.

"Yes," said the Guardian. She tapped her forehead. "In here!" She pointed up the stairs. "Up there you will find the Stacks. You may each choose one book to borrow for one week."

"Aren't books a bit old-fashioned?" asked Arnie.

"Nonsense. A book is a highly complex communication device, involving time travel, telepathy and life after death. It puts you in direct mental communication with the mind of the writer, even if that writer died hundreds of years ago!" The Guardian looked round the group. "Before you go on, I must warn you!"

"What about?" asked Arnie nervously.

"Just now you said you weren't afraid of books. Well, you should be! Books are the most wonderful and terrible things in the world. They can change lives, change history even. If you go up there, you may never be the same again. So, if you are afraid, turn back now, and rejoin the ranks of the empty-headed." The Guardian sighed. "Don't worry, you'll be in the majority."

By now Kim was convinced that the Guardian was crazy, but she wasn't going to refuse a challenge. Empty-headed indeed! "We'll go up," she said. "Won't we?"

"Certainly," said Arnie.

"Why not?" said Sam.

"Good," said the Guardian. She smiled, and suddenly she seemed a lot less frightening. "I knew you were special as soon as I saw you. Good luck!"

"How do we go about choosing the books we want?" asked Sam.

"Don't worry. The books you need will choose you!"

They turned away from the counter and began climbing the stairs. At the top they found themselves faced by a set of double doors.

"Well, here goes," said Kim. She pushed the doors open and they went inside.

They found themselves in an enormous room filled with row after row of bookshelves, stretching away into the distance. It was dimly lit and absolutely silent.

"Doesn't look too dangerous to me," said Sam.

"Or too exciting either," said Arnie.

"Let's just choose our books and get out," said Kim. "We'll meet back here by the door in ten minutes, okay?"

They set off into the endless rows of book-stacks, each one heading in a different direction.

Arnie wandered along the avenues of books feeling fed up. Books, books and more books all around him. How was he supposed to choose just one? A book fell from the shelves, seeming almost to leap out at him. Arnie jumped, then picked the book up and leafed through it. Suddenly the pages began to blur and glow. They became a fiery gateway, drawing him deep inside the book …

He was standing outside a seaside inn, watching a stranger come plodding up to the door. The stranger was a tall, strong, heavy nut-brown man with a tarry pigtail falling over the shoulders of his soiled blue coat. His hands were ragged and scarred with black broken nails and there was a livid white scar across his cheek. He was singing in a high tottering voice: "Fifteen men on the dead man's chest, Yo-ho-ho and a bottle of rum!"

Suddenly it was night and he was in the deserted parlour of the inn, kneeling beside the man's dead body and taking a key that hung round his neck ...

He was upstairs in a bedroom opening an old sea chest with the key, taking out a bundle of papers tied up in oilcloth and a canvas bag that gave out the jingle of gold ...

He was crouched in a ditch, his mother beside him, while cruel ruthless men hunted for them. He knew they would be killed if they were found ...

There were shouts of alarm, the thunder of galloping horses and the screams of a man being ridden down – a blind man called Pew ...

Then he was in a warm, brightly lit room with two men in old-fashioned clothes. One was slender and neat, the other tall, burly and red-faced. The neat man was talking. "Supposing I have here some clue to where Flint buried his treasure, will that treasure amount to much?"

"Amount sir!" cried the other. "It will amount to this: if we have the clue you talk about, I will fit out a ship in Bristol dock and take you and Hawkins here along – and I'll have that treasure if I search a year."

They were opening the oilskin packet of papers. There fell out the map of an island ...

... and found himself pushing open the door of a darkened room and switching on the light. A man lay in the corner of the room, sprawled on his back. There was a long knife through his heart, skewering him to the floor ...

It was the next morning and he was strolling out of a block of flats, disguised as a milkman, whistling cheerily and clanging his milkcans. He knew that the flats were being watched by the killers of his friend – the man called Scudder who had passed on a vital secret before he was murdered. If he was to avoid Scudder's fate, and solve the mystery, he had to get away, far away ...

He was running across bare moorland, desperately looking for shelter from the spotter plane that droned high overhead. Then he saw the line of armed men on the horizon, cutting off his escape. He turned and ran towards the house.

He was in a comfortable study, talking to a bald-headed, kindly-looking old gentleman who was offering him help and shelter. There was something badly wrong.

"This is a lucky morning for you Mr Richard Hannay," said the old man. As he spoke his eyelids seemed to fall a little over his keen grey eyes.

Suddenly he remembered Scudder describing the man he most feared in the world, the man who could hood his eyes like a hawk. He had walked straight into the enemy's headquarters. He turned to run – and saw two men in the doorway covering him with pistols ...

Kim found herself walking steadily towards one particular shelf. She reached up and a book seemed to leap into her hand. Kim flicked through it.

Suddenly she was an unhappy, ill-treated orphan child, driven to defiance, shouting at an older woman. "I am glad you are no relation of mine. I will never call you Aunt again as long as I live. I will never come to see you when I am grown up and if anyone asks me how I liked you and how you treated me, I will say the very

thought of you makes me sick and that you treated me with miserable cruelty … You think I have no feelings and can do without one bit of love or kindness, but I cannot live so."

Years later, a young woman now, she sat studying the strong, harsh face of a man who sat in an armchair by the fire. He looked up.

"You examine me, Miss Eyre. Do you think me handsome?"

"No sir," she replied, and saw his look of astonished amusement. It was the middle of the night and she was in a smoke-filled room, where the man lay fast asleep on a bed with blazing curtains. She seized the water-jug and put out the flames –

She was in a darkened bedroom, caring for the wounds of a mysterious stranger, a man she was forbidden to speak to …

She was in church, about to be married to the man she loved – when a voice from the back of the church called, "The marriage cannot go on!"

They were back at the counter getting their books stamped by the Guardian. She took Arnie's book. "*Treasure Island.* So you choose a life of action and adventure, young man?"

Arnie looked down at his own skinny shape. "Me? I'm no hero!"

The Guardian glared down at him. "The man who wrote that book was a spindly, sickly child. Even when he grew up his health was always bad. But he crossed France by donkey and by canoe, went out to the Far West to find the woman he loved, and sailed his own schooner to the South

Seas." She opened the book, slammed down a big stamp and handed it back to Arnie.

Sam was next. "The Thirty-nine Steps," said the Guardian. "You want excitement and adventure too, but most of all you want to solve problems, crack codes, discover secrets. Well, there are plenty of mysteries in the world to choose from." The stamp slammed down again.

Sam said nothing, but he looked very thoughtful.

Then it was Kim's turn. The Guardian picked up her book. "Jane Eyre. What you want is hardest to find of all. Freedom and independence – and love as well. It can be done, but it isn't easy." She stamped the book and handed it back. "Look after your books," she snapped. "And be back here in one week's time."

"These books," said Arnie.

"What about them?"

"They're not just ordinary books are they? They're – magic!"

"All books are magic, my boy," said the Guardian. She smiled. "But mine are a bit more magic than most!" She disappeared into the shadows.

The three friends collected bike, skateboard and skates and left the Library.

Once outside they stopped and looked at each other.

"I wonder if Jim Hawkins found his treasure?" said Arnie.

"Or if Hannay escaped, and discovered the secret of the thirty-nine steps?" said Sam.

Kim was wondering if Jane Eyre found love and independence. "Well, we know how to find out, don't we?" she said.

Suddenly the once-empty weekend seemed all too short.

"There are thousands of books in there," said Arnie wonderingly.

"Millions!" said Sam.

"We'll come back next week," said Kim.

They set off towards Everytown.

Chapter 3

Spreading the word

When they came to the café where they'd had the lemonade, Kim stopped her bike. "The man said to come back and tell him how we got on."

"Why not?" said Arnie.

Sam remembered the long chase across the moors. "I could do with something to drink – I've had a tiring time!"

They parked their various forms of transport and sat down at the same table as before. As if by magic the café man appeared, carrying a tray with three glasses of lemonade. "Saw you coming."

Kim took a swig of her lemonade. "Aren't you going to ask how we got on?"

"Don't have to," said the man. "You look different."

"How different?" asked Arnie.

"Just different," said the man. "And you've all got books. May I see?" He took the book from Arnie's hand. "Ah, *Treasure Island*! Yo-ho-ho and a bottle of rum! I'll give you a tip – watch out for Long John Silver."

He handed the book back and took the one Sam was carrying. "*The Thirty-nine Steps*," he said softly. "*Greenmantle*, *Mr Standfast*, *Three Hostages*, *Island of Sheep*."

"Come again?" said Sam.

"Books about Richard Hannay. World War One, spies, secret terrorist organisations, master criminals, the lot ...

Did you know old Buchan was a lawyer and a politician and a top civil servant? Worked his way up to be a Lord and ended up Governor of Canada. Wrote a few books on the side for a hobby."

He handed Sam's book back and looked at Kim's, which was older and thicker than the others. "*Jane Eyre*. Now we're on to the hard stuff. There were three of 'em ... "

"Books?" asked Kim, taking back the book.

"Sisters. Lived up on the moors miles from anywhere with a parson father and a drunken brother. Never had much money, never saw much of the world. They all died young, and two out of three wrote masterpieces."

"Have you read everything?" asked Arnie.

The man smiled and shook his head. "No one's read everything. What are you all going to do now?"

Kim shrugged. "Get on with life I suppose. Sunday tomorrow, school on Monday ... "

"What about the others?"

"What others?"

"The ones who need a bit of magic in their lives."

"Are you just going to leave them to it? Or are you going to give them some help?"

"Tell them about the Library you mean?"

"Exactly. Spread the word."

"They'll think we're crazy," said Sam.

"If telling them doesn't work, grab them by the ears and drag them there!"

"Why us?" asked Kim. "Why should we get laughed at?"

The café man leaned over the table. "You can live in books, same as you can live in soap operas or computer games, but that's not really the idea."

"So what is?"

"The idea is to use what you get. Do you think Jim Hawkins would have been scared? Or Dick Hannay? Or Jane Eyre?"

"Very likely they would," said Arnie suddenly. "But they'd have done whatever was needed just the same."

"See?" said the man. "You're learning already!" He started collecting their empty glasses.

"How much for the lemonade?" asked Kim.

"My treat. Special award for people who get past the Guardian. Now remember – spread the word!" He went back inside the café.

They skated, skateboarded and bike-rode through the narrow, twisting streets of Old Town until they reached the bridge that linked the two towns.

In the centre of the bridge they paused, poised between two worlds, looking down at the broad slow river below.

"There's something weird about that café man," said Sam.

"Don't see how he makes any money," said Arnie. "Not if he keeps on giving stuff away."

"I don't think he's all that interested in money," said Kim.

"Are we going to do what he said?" asked Arnie.

"Spread the word, you mean?" asked Sam. "I might give it a go. I can think of someone who needs a bit of help."

Arnie thought for a moment. "Yes ... So can I. How about you, Kim? Can you think of anyone?"

"Yes," said Kim. "I most certainly can ... "

Amy was watching a programme about baboons when her younger brother Chaz came into the room and casually flipped channels on the wall-television. "Don't mind, do you, Amy? Can't stand that nature rubbish!"

He found a football game on satellite and settled down to watch. Amy did mind actually. She was interested in animals. Besides, Chaz could easily have watched sport on the wall-television in his room. But she didn't say anything.

Amy never did. She was a slender, dark-haired girl, always quiet, polite and neatly dressed. Amy never gave any trouble. She decided to go to the computer terminal in her room and tackle her homework. Her mother's voice came out of the wall intercom. "Come and give me a hand getting supper, will you, Amy? You know what people like."

Getting supper in Amy's house, as in many others these days, meant taking foil-wrapped meals from the freezer, putting them in the micro-oven and taking them out when the bell pinged.

"You wouldn't think she'd need any help to do that,' thought Amy. But she didn't say it. "Coming, mother."

Amy went to the big, gleaming white kitchen and started selecting meals, while her mother hovered around watching. Amy took steak and chips for her father, goulash

for her mother, burger and chips for Chaz, and a baby dinner for little Mo. Then she added a meal at random for herself.

Everyone else had their likes and dislikes, but Amy ate anything. As they waited for the food to heat, her mother said, "Oh by the way, Amy, your father and I are going to a residents' committee meeting tonight. You'll look after little Mo, won't you?"

"I'd arranged to meet Kim for a coffee," said Amy.

"You can always give her a call and change it," said her

mother. "I don't understand what you see in that girl anyway. You don't mind, do you?"

"No, I don't suppose you do see why I like Kim," thought Amy. "And as a matter of fact I do mind cancelling. Why can't Chaz baby-sit for once?" But she didn't say anything. Amy never did.

Instead she went up to her neat and tidy room and called Kim on the vidiphone. As the link-up was made she could see Kim in the middle of her amazingly untidy bedroom, studying an odd square object.

"What's that?" asked Amy.

"It's a book," said Kim. "A real book. Some of us went over to Old Town today and had the most amazing time. I'll tell you all about it over coffee."

"I'm afraid I can't make it," said Amy apologetically. "I'm ... "

"Stuck with the baby-sitting as usual," concluded Kim. "You want to get a grip on that family of yours. Well, never mind, if you can't come out, I'll come over to see you. It'll take two of us to control Mo anyway."

The baby's nickname, Mo, was short for Morris – but Kim always insisted it was short for Monster!

"I'm not sure if that's such a good idea," said Amy. "You see my moth ... " Her voice tailed off again.

"Doesn't like me all that much?" said Kim cheerfully. "Well, she'll have to lump me, won't she? Anyway to tell the truth I'm not all that crazy over her. Most crumblies are a pain but yours are worse than most!"

Amy's mother wasn't too pleased when Kim turned up at their house that night. But she was in a hurry to get out to her committee meeting – and as Kim pointed out, she was the one who'd made Amy change her plans.

When they had finally got Mo settled down and asleep, Kim told Amy all about her adventure in Old Town.

"You actually crossed over the river to Old Town?" said Amy.

"That's right. Me and Sam and Arnie."

Amy shuddered. "I could never do anything like that. I'd hate it!"

"That's a pity," said Kim.

"Why?"

"Because you're coming over there with me next Saturday."

"Me? I couldn't!"

"Oh yes you could. I think a trip to the Library will do you a power of good. You need a bit of magic in your life!"

Chapter 4

Buster and Willy

As he skated up to Buster's house, Sam could hear the sound of shouting halfway down the street. First was the voice of Buster's father. "Now see here, these results just aren't good enough, and that's all there is to it. And I don't want to hear any excuses."

"The tests!" thought Sam. The results of the monthly school tests had just been sent to parents. Sam's results had been okay. Buster's hadn't.

The next voice was Buster's. He was shouting just as loud as his father. "You're the one who wants me to be the big sporting hero like you were, in all the school teams. Well, training takes time. I can't do everything."

"You can't do anything, according to these results!"

Next came a female voice – Buster's mum. "Leave the boy alone, can't you?" she screamed. "You're always on at him."

Buster's dad started yelling at her. "You keep out of this. Whenever I try to sort the boy out you interfere."

"Sort him out? That's a laugh. You ignore him for days at a time then yell at him for five minutes. If you took time to be more of a father to him things might be different."

"Oh, so it's all my fault, is it?"

Sam took off his skates and went through the front door. Buster was just storming upstairs, ignored by his parents who were still shouting at each other in the sitting-room.

"And it's not just the children," shrieked Buster's mum, getting into her stride. "I never see you either. Too busy going to conferences with all your chums at United Consolidated."

"I keep telling you, woman, if you want to live this kind of life in this kind of house, I've got to work for it. If you spent a bit less on clothes … "

"If you spent a bit less in the bar of that club of yours … "

"Another quiet night at Buster's place," thought Sam as he followed Buster up to his room – a large, untidy chamber littered with discarded clothes and all kinds of

sporting equipment. When he got there, Buster was yelling again – this time at Zack, his younger brother. "How many times have I got to tell you, stay out of my room and leave my stuff alone! Now hop it!"

"I only wanted to borrow a T-shirt!" screamed Zack. "You're always helping yourself to my stuff."

"I am not!" bellowed Buster.

"No? Well, I'll just have my CDs back, and my jacket ... "

"I told you to clear off – and put that jacket down; it's not yours, it's mine ... "

Grabbing up things as he went, Zack fled from the room. Scowling fiercely, Buster threw himself in his chair. Like his father he was alarmingly large and brawny, dark-haired and very short-tempered.

Zack's mum, on the other hand, was small, dark-haired and bad-tempered – like his sister, who came storming into the room. "Have you pinched my hairbrush again, you horrible hooligan? Yes, there it is!" Snatching it up, she shouted, "Leave my things alone, you light-fingered lout!"

"You'll need more than a hairbrush to do anything with that mop," jeered Buster. "Why don't you get your head shaved and polished?"

Pausing only to chuck a tennis racquet at his head, Buster's sister stormed out again.

Ducking the tennis racquet, Buster seemed to notice Sam for the first time. "Well, what do you want?"

Sam dropped into a chair. "Oh, nothing ... I always come round here when I fancy a bit of peace and quiet and gracious living." Buster jumped to his feet, doubling his fists. "If you've come round here to make cracks about my family ... "

Sam yawned. "Knock it off, Buster. You've had a fight with everyone in the house in the last five minutes. Why add me to the list?"

Buster didn't have many friends, apart from Sam. He didn't have any really, he'd quarrelled with them all. Sam liked Buster for some strange reason, and he simply refused to quarrel. He got up, went to the drink dispenser and dialled a couple of cold cokes. "Here, drink this and cool down."

"Yeah, well," muttered Buster, taking the drink. "It's just that this family drives me crazy. Everyone's so unreasonable. So why did you come?"

Suddenly Sam realised he didn't really know. He had just found himself skating towards Buster's house. Then he remembered the words of the café man: "Spread the word!" If anyone needed a bit of magic in his life it was Buster. But how could he persuade him to go?

"Some of us went over to Old Town earlier," said Sam casually.

"That's a daft thing to do," said Buster. "What's the point?"

"Turned out we had quite an adventure," said Sam. "We're thinking of going back again next Saturday, taking a few friends ... "

"Well, you can count me out."

"Wasn't going to ask you," said Sam. "It was all a bit strange, scary even. You wouldn't like it a bit. You stay over here where it's safe."

"Don't you tell me what to do!" said Buster. "Nothing scares me. Let me know what time you're starting for Old Town and I'll be there!"

Sam grinned. There were ways of handling old Buster …

When Arnie arrived in Willy's room, he found his friend staring at a blank computer screen.

"What's up, Willy?"

"Got some homework to do."

"So do it."

"But I promised Mum I'd tidy my room up."

"Tidy it then."

"What about the homework?"

"Do that after."

"But then I'll be tired and I won't be able to work."

"So do the homework first."

"But if that takes too long I won't have time to tidy. I'll have to stay up late, then I won't be able to work tomorrow."

Willy stood up and started pacing around the room. He was tall and thin with jug-handle ears. His shoulders were stooped, as if he was bowed down by the weight of his worries. "Then there are these test results," he said. "Very worrying."

Sam stared at him. "Willy, you came top!"

"Yes, I know. But suppose I don't do as well next time?

My parents will think I'm not working. Maybe it was just a freak result, maybe I'm going to burn out ... "

Arnie sighed. "Willy, you're bright and you work hard, it's an unbeatable combination. You've got nothing to worry about."

"I haven't been feeling too well lately," said Willy. "Don't seem to have any energy. Maybe my diet's all wrong ... "

"What's wrong is you wear yourself out worrying," said Arnie.

Willy was a full-time worrier. He worried about school, his family, his friends and his health. He worried about mysterious germs lurking in the street, poisonous additives in his food. He worried about world affairs, the ozone layer, the greenhouse effect, the giant panda, dolphins and whales. Not that some of these weren't perfectly sensible worries, thought Arnie. The trouble was, Willy worried about all of them at once and the effort was wearing him out.

"Keep next Saturday free, Willy," ordered Arnie. "You're coming on a little trip with me and Kim and Sam and some others. We're going over to Old Town."

"What?" Willy was horrified. "I'm not going there!"

"Why not?"

"Well, it's old-fashioned and strange and – and probably unhealthy," said Willy.

"I was over there on Saturday, and I haven't come down with anything. Trust me, Willy, it'll be okay. I just have this feeling it'll be good for you."

"All right," said Willy reluctantly. "I'll come." He sat down at his computer again. "Where are we going – when we get to Old Town, I mean?"

"It's better if I don't tell you," said Arnie. "You'd only worry about it … "

Chapter 5

Return to Old Town

Next Saturday morning, Kim, Sam and Arnie were waiting in the plaza. They had abandoned their transport to make it easier for the others.

"Think they'll come?" said Kim.

Sam shrugged. "Who knows?"

"They'd better," said Arnie. "They need to, even if they don't know it."

Amy arrived first. "I'm really not sure about all this," she said. "I don't think my mother would like it."

"Don't tell her then," said Kim.

Amy smiled. "I didn't. I just said we were going for a walk."

"Perfectly true," said Sam. "Look out, here comes Buster."

Buster marched up and towered menacingly over them. "I think this trip to Old Town is a daft idea," he said. "Let's drop it and go to the Civic Park instead."

"Why don't you do that?" said Sam. "There's a nice folk dancing display this morning. I don't think you ought to come to Old Town anyway – you won't like it."

"I'll decide what I like," said Buster. "What are we waiting for?"

"We're waiting for Willy," said Arnie. "Here he comes."

"I really don't feel too well," said Willy when he arrived. "Maybe I'd better not come."

"You never feel well," said Arnie. "You might just as well be ill in Old Town as here. Come on, Willy!"

They set off, walking through the clean, calm streets of Everytown, crossing the bridge and entering the narrow winding streets of Old Town. Amy and Buster and Willy huddled close together, as if they expected the tall, old buildings to fall on top of them.

It was a longish walk and they were tired and thirsty by the time they reached the little café in the square.

"Refreshment stop," said Kim.

As they reached the café the fat, bald café-owner appeared in the doorway. He was carrying a tray with six glasses of lemonade on it. They sat at their usual table and he passed out the lemonade.

"Don't worry," he said to Amy. "You did the right thing coming here." He looked sternly at Buster. "I wouldn't drink it if I were you," he said. "It'll probably disagree with you!"

Buster grabbed the glass and took a defiant swig.

The café man smiled and passed Willy his glass. "Don't worry," he said. "Our lemonade is so strong it kills all known germs!" He went back inside the café.

"That was odd," said Amy.

"How did he know what we were thinking?" said Willy.

"Great lemonade," said Buster when they had all finished. "Wouldn't mind some more."

The café man reappeared. "You can have some more on the way back. Better get a move on, she'll be waiting for you."

"Who will?" asked Amy, but the café man didn't answer.

"How much for the lemonade?" asked Kim.

"No charge," said the café man. "Special offer for first-time visitors – and the people who bring them!"

"You can't make much of a profit giving the stuff away," said Buster.

The café man smiled. "I don't make much of a profit – but I make a very good living."

They went on their way, climbing the steep, narrow street that led up to the Library.

"What's that place?" asked Willy, looking up at the grim, castle-like building towering above them.

"It's the Library," said Kim. "That's where we're going."

They climbed the steps and stood before the huge metal door.

"Well, here we are," said Sam.

"We're going in here?" asked Amy.

"Why?" asked Willy nervously.

"Why not?" said Buster and shoved open the door.

They all went through and the door slammed closed behind them. They found themselves in the same gloomy, marble-floored entrance hall. The same shafts of light came down from the stained-glass windows high in the wall. To the left, the curved flight of stairs led upwards to the stacks. On the far side of the hall, behind the counter of darkly gleaming wood the Guardian stood waiting.

Amy, Buster and Willy looked up in amazement at the tall, grey-haired figure in the shiny black dress. The Guardian peered at them over the gold-rimmed glasses on the end of her long, thin nose, and pointed a bony white finger. "Over here, all of you!"

Footsteps echoing loudly on the marble floor, they made their way over to the counter. The Guardian looked down at them. "New members. Excellent. Hands!"

Amy stared up at her. "What?"

"Just hold your hands out," muttered Kim.

Buster, Amy and Willy held out their hands, palms upwards.

The Guardian examined them and sniffed, just like before.

"I suppose they'll do. Names!"

"Why?" asked Buster boldly.

"Don't waste my time, young man. Names! Addresses!"

Somewhat to his own astonishment Buster heard himself rattling off his full name and address. Amy and Willy did the same. The Guardian wrote them all down in the big leather-covered book, using the same steel-nibbed wooden pen and metal inkwell. When this was done she turned to Kim, Sam and Arnie. "Returned books, please!"

Kim handed over her copy of *Jane Eyre.* The Guardian looked at her. "Well?"

Kim smiled. "Reader, I married him."

The Guardian took the book and put it behind the counter on a shelf marked "Books Just Returned". She took another book from the same shelf. "This was written by Emily, Charlotte Brontë's sister. Charlotte herself said the book was "filled with a horror of great darkness'. Do you think you can deal with it?"

"Yes," said Kim.

The Guardian stamped the book and gave it to Kim. It was called *Wuthering Heights.*

Sam was next. The Guardian took *The Thirty-Nine Steps* and picked up another book. "*Greenmantle*, Richard Hannay's next adventure. A secret mission to Istanbul in the First World War."

"Fine by me," said Sam.

She stamped the book and handed it over.

Arnie returned *Treasure Island* and the Guardian said, "More of the same for you, I think. Not Jim Hawkins but David Balfour. A wicked uncle, Jacobite rebels and a mysterious murder."

She stamped the book and gave it to Arnie. It was called *Kidnapped*. "You three can look at your books in the Reading Room," she said, pointing to a door to the right of the counter. "I shall attend to these three. I can see they need some extra special help ... "

Clutching their books, Kim, Sam and Arnie disappeared through the Reading Room door.

"I'm not sure if I want to be attended to," said Buster. "And I don't need any help either – from you or anyone else."

Unexpectedly the Guardian smiled. "You're a fighter,

young man. It's a good quality … But you don't have to fight everyone and everything all the time."

She looked at Amy and Willy. "And as for you two … " She pointed a long finger at Willy. "You're surrounded by so many imaginary enemies you won't fight at all." The finger swung to Amy. "And you let other people lock you up in prison – because you can't see that the bars are imaginary."

Spreading out her long, bony hands on the wooden counter the Guardian looked thoughtfully at the three children. "Your friends were easy to help. I just had to show them a little of what was already there waiting for them. But you three need special books just for you ... " She shook her head gloomily. "You're putting a strain on my magic. Still, I'll have to try to help you."

She led the way up the stairs ...

Chapter 6

Many adventures

The Reading Room was filled with orderly rows of tables. Each table was surrounded by several chairs, and each had a reading light hanging overhead. The three friends made their way to a table and sat down.

"Wonder how the others are getting on," said Arnie.

"They're in for a bit of a shock," said Kim.

"Do 'em good," said Sam.

They settled down to read.

Arnie was climbing the spiral stairway of a tower in pitch darkness on a stormy night. He had been assured that the stairs were good, but a sudden flash of lightning showed him that they were broken and irregular and that his foot was centimetres from the edge of the stairwell. Suddenly he realised that his uncle, the man who had sent him up the tower was trying to kill him ...

He was on a sailing boat in a harbour, peering over the bulwarks, seeing the rowing boat with his uncle on board, pulling away. He had been tricked – kidnapped!

He gave a piercing cry of "Help, help! Murder!" that rang round the harbour. His uncle turned and showed him a face full of cruelty and terror. A thunderbolt seemed to strike him, he saw a flash of fire and fell unconscious ...

He was in the crowded ship's roundhouse, cutlass in hand fighting for his life with the help of his new friend, a man called Alan Breck. Alan's sword flashed like quicksilver, and soon their enemies were either dead or fleeing for their lives.

"Oh, David," cried Alan, "am I no a bonny fighter?"

Sam was in disguise in the heart of enemy territory, being taunted by a giant of a man called Stumm – a brutal Prussian officer with the build of a gorilla.

"Play me false," said Stumm, "And you had far better never have been born." Stumm's ugly, sneering face loomed over him and two massive hands clamped down on his shoulders in a painful grip. "The weasel would like to bite," cried Stumm. "Stand still, vermin! Smile, look pleasant or I will make pulp of you! Do you dare to frown at me?"

Grinning like an ape, Stumm let him go.

Sam stepped back and hit him straight between the eyes.

"God in heaven!" said Stumm. "I am going to kill you."

He flung himself forward like a mountain …

Kim was telling her companion and servant of her undying love for Heathcliff, the man she could never marry. "He shall never know how much I love him, and that not because he's so handsome but because he's more myself than I am. Whatever our souls are made of, his and mine are the same … "

She was even planning to marry a man she didn't love, so as to help the man she did. "Did it never strike you that if Heathcliff and I married we should be beggars? Whereas if I marry Linton I can aid Heathcliff to rise, and place him out of my brother's power."

It was many years later. She knew she was dying, but she didn't care. She was clasped in the arms of Heathcliff, the man she had always loved. After a long absence he had returned, but it was too late ...

He tried to rise, but she clasped his hair and held him down. "I wish I could hold you till we were both dead. I shouldn't care what you suffered, I care nothing for your sufferings. Why shouldn't you suffer? I do! Will you forget me? Will you be happy when I am in the earth ... "

The Guardian opened the door at the top of the stairs, revealing an enormous room with row upon row of bookshelves stretching away into the distance. "In you go," she said. "The books you need will be waiting for you."

Amy, Buster and Willy were moved slowly through the stacks. Row upon row of books, stretching endlessly into the distance. Amy drifted along in a kind of waking dream, not sure what was real any more. Buster marched ahead, chin up, fists clenched. A lot of mouldy old books weren't going to scare *him* ...

Willy was terrifed and didn't care who knew it. This place was enormous – suppose they got lost in here?

They came to a crossroads in the stacks, but they didn't hesitate. It was as if they knew where they had to go. Amy turned to the left, and Willy to the right. Buster, of course, marched boldly onward.

The Guardian's words seemed to echo in all their minds. Somewhere ahead their books were waiting for them.

Amy found herself in a quiet alcove. She stretched out her hand and a book seemed almost to float into it. Its brightly coloured cover showed a dark girl in a long white dress, clasped in the arms of a handsome soldier. "Some trashy romance,' thought Amy disapprovingly. She opened the book ...

She was the girl in the white dress, covered now by a travelling-cloak, and she was hurrying along cobbled streets. From somewhere in the distance came the rumble of gunfire. The street was full of little groups of people, talking uneasily.

Not far away, near a little village called Waterloo, a great battle was being fought – and no one yet knew who had won or lost. Brussels was filled with all kinds of rumours. Some said that the English had already lost, pointing out that Napoleon, the great French leader, had never really been defeated.

A line of carts swung around the corner, each one filled with weary, mud-covered men – rough, blood-soaked bandages around terrible wounds. Their faces were haggard and pale, but they tried to smile and look cheerful. One or two waved feebly at the onlookers. Some called feebly for water. Most just lay there, too weak and dazed to move.

English wounded brought back from the battlefield. "Perhaps we've lost after all,' she thought.

A voice at her elbow said, "Poor fellows! They've set up hospital tents for them at the Naumur Gate."

She turned and saw her friend Kate, a tall, sharp-faced girl with untidy hair. "We've got to help them," Kate went on. "They need all the lint and linen we can find, sheets for bandages, medicines … I'm going to collect up everything I can find and go round to help the doctors. Are you coming, Amelia?"

"Me? I couldn't. Mother's making arrangements for us to leave … "

"Scuttling off?" said Kate scornfully. "How could you? Besides there's no need. The Duke will settle Boney for us."

The Duke was the Duke of Wellington, the English commander. "Mother says the Duke has never faced Napoleon before. Only his generals."

"Well, he saw them off and he'll see Boney off too," said Kate loyally. "Now, I must be going. I'll be expecting you at the Naumur Gate. Don't let me down!"

"It's different for Kate," thought Amelia, as she hurried on her way. Kate had lost her mother when she was young, and she had travelled all over Spain and Portugal with her soldier father. She was used to war and battles.

Amelia's father was a soldier too, but she had stayed at home with her mother and her brothers and sisters. Only when Napoleon had been, as it seemed, defeated had she been allowed to come with her mother, who was joining her father in Brussels. Like most English people Amelia had been unable to travel abroad before. The war with Napoleon had been going on all her life. Then suddenly it was peace and the English flocked abroad. Amelia had enjoyed the adventure enormously, even though she knew she had only been brought along as her mother's companion and unpaid servant.

"Such a practical girl, Amelia," her mother always said. "So *useful* ... "

Now it had all turned into a nightmare. Like some monster that refused to die, Napoleon had broken free from his captivity, rallied the French around him, and returned to the attack.

Amelia went up the steps of the big house they had rented in a fashionable square, gave her cloak to the waiting butler and went upstairs to the luxuriously furnished first-floor sitting-room.

Her mother was pacing anxiously to and fro. "There you are at last Amelia! Where have you been? How can you be so selfish?" As usual she rattled on without waiting for an answer. "I've told your maid to pack for you. We shall leave as soon as she is finished." She tugged at the bell-rope and after a moment the butler hurried into the room. "Have the carriage brought around at once, Pierre. We shall be leaving immediately."

Amelia thought of what lay ahead. The long coach journey along refugee-crowded roads, with her mother complaining all the way. The passage back to England in some overcrowded ferry. The long wait for news of her father – and of Harry …

She saw the patient, weary faces of the wounded soldiers as the carts jolted over the cobbles. She heard a firm voice say, "No. I'm not going." To her astonishment the voice was her own.

"I beg your pardon, Amelia?" Her mother's voice was frozen with outrage.

Amelia didn't care. She turned to the astonished butler. "Tell my maid to stop unpacking, I shall not be leaving. Then tell the servants to collect all the linen in the house – sheets, blankets, pillows, anything that might be useful. Pack it all up into some kind of cart, there's bound to be one in the stables, and send it round to me at the hospital tent at the Naumur Gate."

"At once, Miss Amelia." The butler hurried off.

"I know the reason for this nonsense," said her mother suddenly. "It's that Captain Vaughan, isn't it? The one you danced almost every dance with at the Duchess of Richmond's ball. You're besotted with him!"

Amelia's mind went back to last night's ball, the great event of the Brussels social season. The scarlet and gold of the uniforms, the blues and greens and whites of the ballgowns …

Harry Vaughan's uniform had been green though. "Because I'm a rifleman," he explained proudly. He was slim and dark with a beaky nose and a lively, cheerful face. Amelia smiled. Had it been love at first sight? Liking certainly, and laughter as well. His flow of cheerful talk had drawn her out, made her forget her usual shyness. She wasn't sure what he felt about her – but he *had* asked her for every available dance …

"It isn't about Captain Vaughan," she told her mother. "Or perhaps it is. Him and all the other soldiers who may need help. I must go."

The hospital tent was an overcrowded nightmare. The flood of wounded from the battlefield seemed unending, the Belgian doctors desperately overworked. Amelia helped to dress wounds that would once have made her faint even to look at. She tore up sheets to make bandages. She fed sips of water to desperately wounded men. She was aware of Kate working nearby, a scowl of determination on her face. "Well done," whispered Kate, as she passed by with a fresh pile of bandages.

Amelia was too tired to reply.

The flood of wounded died down at last, and there was time for a moment's rest. "Here," said Kate and passed her a glass of wine and water. It was thin and sour, but to the parched Amelia it tasted wonderful.

Suddenly a familiar voice snapped, "Amelia!" She turned and saw her father marching towards her, her mother on his arm. He looked weary but seemed to be unhurt. He wasn't pleased. "What is the meaning of this Amelia?" he barked.

Before Amelia could say anything, one of the doctors answered for her. He was a stocky, middle-aged Belgian with grizzled grey hair. "The meaning, mon colonel, is that this young lady, with many others, has worked for long hours to help those who have suffered in your precious battle. She has been as brave as any soldier. You have no reason to reproach her. You should be proud of her."

Amelia's father wasn't used to being spoken to in this tone. For a moment he stiffened. Then he relaxed and smiled wearily. "You are quite right, doctor. I should be proud, and I am. Well done, my dear." To Amelia's astonishment he put his free arm round her and gave her a hug. Amelia saw that her mother was crying and kissed her tear-stained cheek.

Then, over her mother's shoulder, she saw a thin, green-uniformed soldier at the entrance of the tent, talking to Kate. He looked grimy and exhausted and one arm was in a sling.

"Harry!" she called. Pulling away from her parents, she ran over to him. He put his good arm round her and bent down to kiss her.

"Such a victory, Amelia," he said excitedly. "Boney's beaten at last." His expression changed to one of sadness. "But at such a cost – so many good friends gone … "

"But your arm … "

"Just a scratch, it's nothing … I called at your house as soon as I got back, and they told me you were here. I knew you'd do something like this."

"More than I did," said Amelia. "It's all thanks to Kate here." She looked at the two smiling figures on the other side of the tent. "I think you'd better come and meet the family. They're not so bad when you get to know them … "

Chapter 7

Trail drive to Tombstone

Buster marched through the seemingly endless stacks of books, glaring fiercely around him. He didn't like this place, didn't like the Guardian and the bossy way she talked to them. No one was going to scare him with a lot of mystical mumbo jumbo. He came to a dead end, a wall of books barring his way. Buster reached out and grabbed a book as if he intended to throttle it. He opened it at random ...

... and he was in the saddle of a tired horse, galloping along the edge of a huge herd of long-horned cattle. For some reason the herd had come to a stop, and the worried cattle were milling uneasily to and fro.

He came up beside one of the trail-hands, who was riding up and down the herd, trying to quieten the nervous animals. "What's the delay?" he yelled. "We've gotta get them cattle across the river if we're gonna make Tombstone by tomorrow."

"Indians," called the cowboy. "Holding us up at the ford."

"Not for long they ain't," growled Buster. He spurred his weary horse and rode on. The herd had come to a

halt where the river narrowed a little. According to their map this was the only crossing point for miles.

A little group of Indians on scraggy ponies huddled at the river's edge talking to the outfit's scout – a tubby, bald-headed, old man known simply as the Old Timer.

He studied the Indian band. There were half a dozen at most, young braves led by one much older man who wore the plumed head-dress of a chief.

"Don't seem too many of them,' he thought. "May be more in hiding.' He had fought Indians before and he knew the almost miraculous way in which they could appear from nowhere in an apparently empty prairie.

He rode up to the little group. "What's the delay?"

"It's these Indians, boss," said the Old Timer. "According to the chief here we gotta hand over some cattle – "

"The hell we have!" snapped Buster. "I didn't bring these cows all the way from Texas just to hand 'em over to a bunch of Indians. Move the herd across. And tell those Indians to get out of the way or get trampled!"

"But boss – "

"Don't argue, do as I say! Tell him, Old Timer."

The Old Timer spoke a few guttural words, reinforcing them with sign language. His last gesture, a cutting motion with his flat hand, was unmistakable.

The chief turned and looked at Buster for a moment, his eyes like black stones in the brown wrinkled face. Then he turned his pony and rode away, the braves trotting after him.

"See?" said Buster. "You just gotta let 'em see you won't stand no nonsense. Now, let's move them cattle."

It took several hours of hard, sweaty work to get the herd of longhorns across the river. It was dark by the time the job was finished. They made camp on the other side and the cowhands relaxed, looking forward to food and sleep. The cook started banging on an iron pot with a wooden spoon and the hungry crew gathered round the chuckwagon.

Then the raiders struck. Suddenly the camp was filled with mounted men, yelling and firing, stampeding the cattle. Not Indians, though, white men with hats pulled low and bandannas pulled up to cover their faces.

Buster grabbed for the Colt .45 in his holster, but even as he cocked it he saw one of the mounted men levelling an enormous rifle at him. He felt a hammer-blow in the chest and fell backwards into the water …

He opened his eyes to see clouds swirling in a night sky. He was floating on his back in the shallows at the river's

edge. Everything was quiet, no lowing cattle, no shooting, no yelling. Just the eerie sighing of the night wind through the cottonwood trees along the river.

He heard a slow clop of hoofbeats. A shadow fell across him and he saw a towering shape outlined against the night sky. It was a man on horseback. To his astonishment he saw that it was the Old Timer.

"It don't have to be like this, son," said the old man.

"It don't?" said Buster feebly.

"Nope. Most often there's another way."

Leaning down from the saddle the Old Timer stretched out a hand. He reached out and the old man pulled him up. Once on his feet he looked down at his chest, patting it cautiously. He had been shot at close range by a Sharp's buffalo rifle. By rights he should have a hole in him the size of a dinner plate. But he seemed to be quite unharmed …

A riderless horse trotted up. It was *his* horse.

"Mount up, son," said the Old Timer. "Let's try her again … "

Impatiently he rode up to the little group at the river's edge. "What's the delay, Old Timer?"

"It's these Indians, boss. Chief here wants us to hand over some cattle – "

Buster felt a surge of rage inside him. With a mighty effort, he managed to control it. Keeping his face expressionless he said, "How many?"

The Old Timer barked out a guttural question. The chief held up one hand, fingers spread.

"Five!" Buster almost laughed. Five – out of five thousand. "Ask him how come?"

There was another brief exchange and the Old Timer said, "Seems like it's a kind of tax, boss, on account of the river crossing's on Indian land. All the herds hand over a few steers. Chief says there's a village of his people a few miles downriver. Women and kids mostly, and they're all pretty hungry. Hunting's bad since the white man killed off all the buffalo. According to the peace treaty, Government's supposed to give 'em food – but it comes late if it comes at all."

Buster looked at the old chief's face, the unblinking eyes like black stones set in the wrinkled, leathery face. "All this land was theirs once," he thought. "We killed off the buffalo they live on, broke all our promises, penned them up in reservations. Now he's down to begging for a few steers to keep his people alive."

"Tell the chief five steers is too few for a hungry village," he said. "Tell him to take ten."

The Old Timer relayed the message and, just for a moment, a flicker of surprise passed over the old chief's face. He spoke again at some length this time, and when the deep voice came to an end Old Timer translated. "Chief says there are men hiding in the cottonwood grove just round the bend on the other side of the river. One of his braves spotted them when he was out hunting."

"What do they want – to tax the herd as well?"

The Old Timer shook his head. "Nope. They plan to kill us all and steal the herd."

"The whole herd?"

"Seems they leave the big drives alone, too many on guard. But a small outfit like ours … "

Buster sat silently on his horse, taking in the new threat.

The Old Timer went on. "Chief says there's another crossing, near his village, not marked on the maps."

He thought hard, a plan forming in his mind. "Tell Chief we'll need his help. Tell him it's worth another ten cows."

It was near to dawn when they got the last of the herd across the ford by the Indian village. They brought them across in bunches, each one guided by an Indian brave. All the time they had kept a big fire burning by the chuckwagon at the original crossing. Buster hoped the watching bandits wouldn't realise the main herd was growing smaller and smaller

When the crossing was complete, they thanked the chief, gathered the herd and moved away.

It was later in the day when they saw the riders, about a dozen of them galloping towards them, strung out in a line.

Buster turned to his men. "Sit quiet, but be ready."

The leader rode up to him, a wolfish grin on his unshaven face.

"Pretty sneaky cowboy – and after we waited all morning for you at the ford. Still, we caught up in the end."

"Might be healthier if you hadn't."

The bandit leader snatched out a gun – and slumped from his saddle, an arrow in his chest.

As their leader fell from his saddle, the next bandit grabbed for his gun – and froze at the double click as Buster cocked and aimed the Winchester rifle that lay across his saddle. All the rest of the cattle drovers had guns in their hands.

"Every man's covered," said Buster flatly. "Ride or die."

The bandits wheeled and galloped away.

Buster looked in the direction from which the arrow had come. For an instant he saw the Indian chief on his pony, silhouetted against the skyline. Then the figure disappeared.

"World's full of troubles," said the Old Timer. "Helps to make a few friends along the way … "

Buster closed the book, and found himself back in the stacks. "Well, maybe," he thought. "Things could have worked out like that. All the same, those were dangerous times. Better not to back down … "

He opened the book again.

He was riding through a lonely graveyard on the outskirts of town. Faded wooden crosses leaned drunkenly against the skyline. Buster leaned down from his horse to read the pencilled inscription on a new cross.

Zack Thackery, Horse Thief

'He died of a fatal case of slow!'

Leaving Boot Hill behind him, he rode on down into Tombstone. It was early evening. Most of the saloons and gambling joints were still closed. From one of them came the feeble tinkling of an ancient piano.

He rode on into the better part of town and pulled up outside a fancy hotel called the 'Tombstone Palace'. He swung down from his horse, hitched it to the tie-rail, pushed open the bat-wing doors and went into the bar.

Except for a few early drinkers, the long cool room was empty. At the far end was a long mahogany bar with a bored bartender polishing glasses. He marched across to the bar, his boots noisy on the polished wooden floor.

"Beer!" he said.

He watched thirstily as the bartender filled the mug from the barrel. A voice said quietly, "You're over the deadline, cowboy."

He turned and saw two men playing cards at a table near the end of the bar. The one who had spoken was a tall, thin man in a black suit. He had a long, melancholy face with a drooping moustache. His opponent was smaller, thin-faced, coughing as he shuffled a pack of cards.

"Come again?"

"You're in the respectable part of town, past the deadline. Around here you check your guns at the marshal's office – *before* you come into the bar."

"Listen, mister, I've just brought a herd of cattle through hell and high water, not to mention bandits and Indians and no tinhorn gambler is going to tell me to take off my gun – "

"Hold it, cowboy!"

It was the second cardplayer, still coughing as the cards flowed through his hands. "Something you ought to know."

"Yeah, what?"

"You're talking to Wyatt Earp."

The tall man stood up and stepped away from the table, brushing back the right side of his black coat. The action revealed the marshal's star on his chest, and the handle of the long-barrelled Colt at his side.

Suddenly conscious of the weight of the holstered Colt at his side, the newcomer wiped a hand across dry lips. "So what? Where's my beer?"

"Go check your gun, cowboy."

"The hell I will!"

The other cardplayer coughed. "Just check it, kid. Marshal's office is right across the street."

Buster swallowed. "And if I don't?"

The marshal said, "You've been warned. Any man comes over the deadline wearing a gun comes against me."

There was a long, long pause. Everything was absolutely quiet. Then Buster went for his gun. There didn't seem to be anything else he could do. Even before his gun cleared the holster, the long-barrelled Colt in Earp's hand boomed just once, and the heavy bullet hammered Buster to the ground.

As the blackness started to close over him, he heard Earp say sadly, "Damn-fool kid."

The man called Doc said, "Supply never runs out, does it? A fresh batch with every trail herd."

"You saw, Doc," said Wyatt Earp sadly. "He drew on me. What could I do?"

"Not a thing," said Doc Holliday. "Charlie – send for the undertaker. We've got another customer for Boot Hill."

When Buster opened his eyes he was staring at the sky from the bottom of a shallow grave. He looked up and saw the Old Timer squatting by the grave side.

"Some folks take a heap of convincing. You could have played it another way."

"I could?"

The Old Timer reached out a hand and helped him out of the grave. He saw, with no great surprise, that he seemed to be unhurt and that his horse was waiting patiently by the graveside. He swung into the saddle …

He was riding through the streets of Tombstone, getting down outside the Tombstone Palace and going inside. "Beer, bartender."

A quiet voice said, "You're over the deadline, cowboy."

He turned and saw a tall man in a dark suit playing cards at a table near the end of the bar. He had a long, melancholy face with a drooping moustache. His opponent was smaller, thin-faced, coughing as he shuffled a pack of cards.

"Come again?"

"You're in the respectable part of town, past the deadline. Around here you check your guns at the marshal's office – *before* you come into the bar."

"Always helps to know who you're dealing with," thought Buster. Cautiously he said, "And you'd be?"

The tall man stood up and stepped away from the table, brushing aside his black coat, revealing the star on his chest, and the handle of the long-barrelled Colt at his side. "Wyatt Earp, City Marshal."

Buster wiped lips that suddenly seemed even drier. "Well, I'll tell you Mr Earp, I've been looking forward to that cold beer for many a mile. If you'll give me a minute to drink it, I'll head straight for your office and check my gun – and I'll make sure my boys go there first when they come into town."

There was a long, long pause. Everything was absolutely quiet. Then the marshal said, "Sounds reasonable to me. I'll even buy you the beer. Give the man his drink, Charlie."

The bartender slid the foaming mug along the bar. Buster grabbed it and drained it in one long swallow. He touched the brim of his Stetson. "Obliged, marshal."

He clumped across to the bat-wing doors. Behind him he heard the coughing man say, "Well, he sure faced you down, Wyatt!"

He heard Earp chuckle. "Good kid – guts *and* good manners. Rare combination!"

Outside in the street Buster pushed back his hat and mopped his brow. It was pretty nice not being dead. He led his horse across the street to the marshal's office.

Chapter 8

One for all

Willy moved cautiously between the stacks. He had suddenly discovered he was all alone, and he didn't like it one bit. Suppose he got lost in here? He just couldn't understand how the place could be so *big*. The stacks alone seemed to be immense, like a forest. Surely the Library wasn't bigger on the inside than on the outside?

Suddenly he saw a book on the floor at his feet. As he bent to pick it up, it seemed to open in his hands ...

... and he found himself in an ornately decorated chamber, rising from a deep formal bow. The man he had been bowing to – a portly type in elaborate old-fashioned clothes – said, "Welcome to the Musketeers, young man. I'm sure you will do us credit."

Willy bowed again, backed out of the room – and bumped into a wiry, young man in the tunic of a musketeer, who was hurrying along the corridor. He had a dark, rakishly handsome face. "Can't you look where you're going, fellow?" the man snapped.

"I regret any inconvenience, monsieur. If you are still dissatisfied, you have only to name a time and place." Instinctively his hand dropped to the hilt of the long sword that hung at his hip.

"What am I saying?" thought Willy, the real Willy. But he didn't seem to be able to control this other self.

Unexpectedly the stranger threw back his head and laughed. "Just joined the Musketeers?"

"I have that honour."

"And all ready for a duel on your first day! Well, I did much the same myself. In fact I had three arranged in no time!"

He held out his hand. "D'Artagnan. Welcome to the Musketeers."

Willy returned the handshake. "Guillaume d'Estragon."

"From Gascony?"

"Normandy."

"Hah, a cold-blooded northerner!"

Somehow Willy knew that Gascons were from the south, famous for poverty, pride and fiery tempers.

"Never mind, not your fault," D'Artagnan went on. "We'll celebrate your joining with a flagon or two of wine in the 'King's Arms'. Your treat, I'm afraid, I'm penniless till payday! Guillaume's a bit of a mouthful, isn't it?"

"Call me Willy if you like."

"Come along then, Veelee," said D'Artagnan.

Willy found it impossible to argue with his forceful new friend. At the head of the big staircase in the entrance hall they were held up by a noisy group of musketeers. They seemed to be playing a highly dangerous form of King of the Castle. One stood at the head of the stairs, sword drawn, taking on three others at once. The air was filled with the clash of steel and the excited shouts of the spectators.

"When he's wounded, the man who wounded him takes his place," explained D'Artagnan. "We'll nip past during the changeover – unless you'd care to join in, Veelee?"

"Later, perhaps," said Willy hurriedly.

The man at the top of the stairs dropped his sword, clutching a wounded wrist. There was a roar of laughter, and they slipped past while the next man took his place.

They went down the stairs, across a courtyard and out into a cobbled, tree-lined square. D'Artagnan marched him towards a crowded, noisy tavern, packed with laughing, drinking, quarrelling musketeers.

It was the sort of place that Willy, the real Willy, couldn't stand, and he struggled to gain some control over things. "Looks a bit overcrowded," he said. He looked round and saw a smaller, quieter tavern on the other side of the square. "Why don't we go over there?"

D'Artagnan stared at him. "You want us to go and have a drink in the 'Cross of Lorraine'?"

"Why not?"

"Why not indeed? No D'Artagnan ever refused a challenge!"

They crossed the square and went into the other tavern. It was much like the first – stone floor, wooden benches and tables, a bar at the end. But it was much quieter – the only other customers were a little group of men in blue cloaks at a table by the door, talking in low voices.

Pleased with his choice, Willy ordered wine for them both. The innkeeper looked strangely at him but poured two tankards. Willy paid for them.

D'Artagnan chose an empty table in a dark corner. He still seemed uneasy, keeping his back to the wall and looking cautiously around him.

The tavern started to fill up, until almost every table was full. The customers were a grim, stern-looking lot, quite unlike the cheerful, rowdy musketeers. The odd thing was that they *all* seemed to be wearing blue cloaks with a cross on the back.

"Maybe it's some sort of club," thought Willy.

He pointed this out to D'Artagnan, who stared at him as if he were mad.

"Nom de chien, of course they're all dressed the same. They're the Cardinal's Guards. We're drinking in *their* tavern."

Some very unwelcome information was flooding into Willy's mind. The Cardinal was Cardinal Richelieu, the King's chief minister, the most powerful man in France.

The King's Musketeers and the Cardinal's Guards were deadly rivals. What he had done was the equivalent of going into a Millwall supporters' pub wearing Arsenal colours.

"Feelings are running pretty high at the moment," said D'Artagnan.

Willy gulped. "Why's that?"

"Well, it's my fault really. I got into a bit of a scuffle with the Cardinal's Guards the other night."

"A bit of a scuffle?"

"There were four of us and seven of them. Two ran away and the other five are in hospital."

"Wonderful!" thought Willy. "Not just in the wrong pub in the wrong colours, but on a night when the other side's just suffered a humiliating defeat. I'm doomed!"

Echoing his thoughts, D'Artagnan said, "Luckily they haven't noticed us yet."

"And when they do?"

"We'll be lucky to get out of here alive!"

Willy sighed. "No use putting it off. We'd better make a move."

He stood up – and everything went wrong. He had intended to sidle quietly towards the door, hoping no one would notice him, but somehow his story self took over. That self seemed determined to prove that he was as much of a daredevil as any musketeer in the regiment. He went up to the bar and slammed down his tankard.

"More wine, landlord," he shouted. "And mind you give us something decent this time. This vinegar might do for the Cardinal's Guards, but it's not fit for a musketeer!"

A tall, scar-faced guard leaped to his feet, hand on his sword. "You object to our taste in wine, monsieur?"

"I object to your taste in so many things. The uniform you wear, the treacherous master you choose to serve. But the wine really is very bad. Try it!"

He threw the remnants of the wine in the guard's face, and leaped back, reaching for his sword.

"Veelee!" shouted D'Artagnan. "The table!"

He grabbed one end of the table they had been sitting at and D'Artagnan took the other. Using the heavy table as a combined shield and battering ram, they forced their way through the angry and astonished crowd.

Once outside, they dropped the table and ran across the square, angry guards at their heels like a pack of wolves. D'Artagnan headed straight for the 'King's Arms' yelling, "Musketeers! Musketeers!"

Summoned by the rallying cry, three musketeers appeared in the doorway of the tavern. One was handsome and aristocratic with a pale, proud face. The second was a moustachioed giant of a man who wore a faded blue coat with ragged gold embroidery instead of a tunic. His enormous sword was supported on a

splendid gold belt. The third was a good-looking, young man with a thin moustache and a mild, scholarly air.

"Athos! Porthos! Aramis!" shouted D'Artagnan.

"In trouble again, D'Artagnan?" drawled Athos.

"Not my fault, I swear," said D'Artagnan. "It's Veelee here. Never known such a fire-eater!"

The pursuing guards had caught up with them by now, and found themselves facing not two but five musketeers.

"Won't you join us for a drink in *our* tavern?" said D'Artagnan mockingly. "I can promise you a warm reception – and some decent wine!"

The musketeers drew their swords, so did the guards. Soon the little square was filled with the rattle of steel. Willy found himself facing a massive guardsman who charged straight at him like a bull, brandishing his sword. But there was more strength than science in the attack, and to his relief Willy found that his other self was an expert swordsman who could handle his opponent with ease.

A lunge, a parry, another lunge, a turn of the wrist – and the guard's sword flew from his hand. The man turned and ran, and Willy turned to look for another opponent.

Athos, Porthos, Aramis and D'Artagnan were all fully engaged, and didn't need any help. Athos fought with a calm, deadly precision, driving his opponent steadily back. Porthos, on the other hand, teased his opponent with a flow of cheerful chatter, jokes, bits of court gossip, insults … Unfortunately the poor man was too out of breath to reply. Aramis fenced with an air of mild abstraction, as if composing a poem in his head.

D'Artagnan fought with a wild exuberance, more than making up for his lack of size and weight with an almost acrobatic agility. He quickly ran his opponent through his sword arm, and the man's weapon clattered on the cobblestones.

Suddenly a voice shouted, "Stop! Put up your swords, gentlemen, or you will be arrested."

It was the tall, scar-faced man in whose face Willy had thrown the wine. He had arrived with an overwhelming force of guards behind him. He bowed stiffly. "I am the Captain of the Cardinal's Guard. Unfortunately it is part of my duties to enforce the laws against public brawling. Sheathe your swords, gentlemen, or accompany me to the Bastille."

Guardsmen and musketeers sheathed their swords and the two groups slowly separated.

The Guard Captain looked hard at Willy. "I trust I shall have the pleasure of meeting you again very soon."

"You have only to name the time and place," said Willy grandly.

The Guard Captain turned away and the rest of the guards followed.

"Have a care, young man," boomed Porthos. "That's Biscarrat, one of the finest swordsmen in the guards. I've had a bout or two with him myself."

"Oh that won't worry Veelee!" said D'Artagnan, throwing an arm round Willy's shoulders and leading him into the 'Cross of Lorraine'. "Nothing scares Veelee! Did you see the way he disarmed poor old de Jussac?"

"Everything scares me really," thought Willy, as they went into the tavern. But it was nice having people think he was a hero. They made their way to a table by the door, and D'Artagnan told his friends of their meeting.

"He picks a fight with me – *me* – the minute he's a musketeer. Then he insists on having a drink in a tavern full of guards. Not content with that he insults their wine, their uniform and the Cardinal himself, and flings the rest of his wine in Biscarrat's face."

"Reckless to the point of madness!" said Aramis. "He'll make an excellent musketeer!"

"We should celebrate his arrival amongst us properly," said Porthos. "A good dinner at least. Unfortunately I couldn't resist this piece of finery … " He tapped the gold belt that supported his sword.

"Don't turn to me," said D'Artagnan. "Bad luck at cards."

"Or me," said Aramis. "A very expensive young lady."

"No gentleman cares to discuss money," said Athos grandly.

"Never mind that," roared Porthos. "Have you got any?"

"No. The last of my funds bought the last of our wine."

They all looked hopefully at Willy. He knew that the rest of the money in his purse was supposed to last him the rest of the month. But then again, the way things were going, he probably wouldn't even live that long.

The wonderful thing was, he didn't care. Just for once, Willy wasn't worried – about anything. He took the purse from his pocket and tossed it on the table. "I hope, gentlemen, that you will consent to be my guests for the evening."

Porthos grabbed the purse. "I'll go and order dinner!"

"Wait," said D'Artagnan. "First, a toast."

They called for more wine, and when it arrived, they clinked their tankards together.

"All for one!" cried D'Artagnan. "And one for all!"

Together they repeated the cry.

"All for one – and one for all!"

Chapter 9

Changing times

"No!" said Willy suddenly. He slammed the book shut, thrust it back on the shelves and ran between the stacks, going back the way he had come.

To his surprise he found the stairs without any trouble. The others – Kim, Sam, Arnie, Buster and Amy – were all waiting for him, books under their arms. The Guardian was there too, brandishing her stamp.

"Where's your book, young man?"

"I haven't got one," said Willy. "I couldn't find anything I liked."

"I'm sorry you couldn't find something to suit you. Come back again another time and we'll try again."

"Something about birdwatching maybe," said Buster. "If that's not too exciting."

"Knock it off, Buster," said Amy suddenly. "Leave him alone."

Buster gave her an astonished look and said mildly, "Sorry Willy. Nothing wrong with birdwatching."

Kim and Sam looked at each other.

"Fancy Amy getting tough," whispered Kim.

"And Buster being reasonable," said Sam.

"Pity about poor Willy," said Arnie.

"Come on, you lot," said Kim. "Let's go home."

They said goodbye to the Guardian and left the Library.

The Guardian watched them go, looking regretfully at Willy who trailed off sadly behind the rest. "Maybe the Musketeers were a bit much for him," she said to herself. "Ah well, can't win 'em all! Perhaps it did him *some* good."

They stopped for lemonade on their way back through Old Town. As usual the café man seemed to be expecting them. He looked at their books – Kim's *Wuthering Heights*, Sam's *Greenmantle*, Arnie's *Kidnapped* – and nodded approvingly. He looked at Buster's *Wild West Tales* and Amy's *Heroine of Waterloo*. "Haven't read those – they look interesting though."

They all finished their lemonades and started getting ready to leave. The café man turned to Willy who sat sadly, sipping at his lemonade. "Where's your book, young man?"

"Haven't got one," muttered Willy. "I couldn't find one I liked. Or rather, I didn't like the one I found ... I couldn't handle it."

"I'm very sorry to hear that," said the café man. His voice was curiously sympathetic. "Tell me about it."

Willy told him about the Musketeers book.

"Suddenly it all got too much for me."

"What did exactly?"

Willy gave him a worried look. "The way those people lived – the ones in the book, I mean. It was mad, quite mad."

"Was it?"

"They played dangerous games with swords, they got into fights all the time on the slightest excuse, they threw away their money on fancy clothes and wine. They didn't seem to worry about *anything*. You can't live like that."

"Not today, you can't," agreed the café man. "Maybe you never could. Your Musketeers are a bit of a fantasy after all. But I think you're a bit hard on them all the same. They had some admirable qualities."

"They did?"

"They were brave and loyal and cheerful and they helped one another. As for not worrying about anything – is it any worse than going through life worrying about everything?"

"I don't know," said Willy. He finished his lemonade and went off with the others.

As Amy went back into her house she heard her Mother call, "Amy, where have you been? Come and help me with supper, will you."

"Sorry, Mum," yelled Amy. "Something I want to see on television. Try one of the others. It's their turn anyway, for about the next five years!"

The only reply was an astonished silence.

Amy went into the sitting-room and switched on the wall-television. A programme about badgers was just beginning.

Her brother Chaz came into the room, grabbed the remote and switched channels. "Sorry, sis, football."

Amy snatched the remote from his hand and changed the channel back. "Sorry, bro, badgers! You can watch football in your room."

He tried to grab the remote and she gave him a rap on the knuckles with it that made him yell in astonishment.

"I'll tell Mum," he threatened.

"You'll find her in the kitchen," said Amy. "As a matter of fact she needs someone to help with supper."

There was one curry and one chicken dinner left when Amy and her brother came into the dining-room. Amy took the chicken.

"I wanted that one," protested her brother.

"Tough," said Amy. "I don't like curry."

"You used to eat it. You used to eat anything."

"Times have changed," said Amy.

Her father, a quiet man who never said much because he never got a chance to, looked thoughtfully at her but said nothing.

After supper her mother said, "Will you babysit for me tonight, Amy?"

"I'm afraid I can't," said Amy. "I'm going over to Kim's house."

"But I've got a social committee meeting, and your father's going out too. What am I going to do?"

"One of three things," said Amy. "Find someone else, take Mo with you, or stay home."

"But you always used to babysit," wailed her mother.

"I still will," said Amy. "But not tonight. Any other time, all you need to do is ask me – in advance."

Later that night when she got home from her meeting – she'd had to bribe Amy's brother to babysit – Amy's mother said, "You know, I'm getting a bit worried about Amy. She was acting so strangely tonight."

"I used to be worried about Amy myself," said Amy's father. "But I'm not any more."

When Buster came into his room, his younger brother Zack was rooting around in his clothes cupboard. "Looking for anything special?" asked Buster amiably.

"Sorry Buster," mumbled Zack, preparing to dodge the expected clip on the ear. "Rock show at the Civic Theatre, got nothing to wear."

"Why not take the Mickey Mouse T-shirt?" suggested Buster. "That's so old-fashioned it's trendy again." He

fished the shirt from under a pile and tossed it over. "Keep it if you like, I never wear it these days."

His brother backed cautiously away. "You feeling all right, Buster?"

"Never better," said Buster. He fished a crumpled ten-credit note from his back pocket. "Here, have a rave-up on me!"

His brother took the money, muttered his thanks and ran.

As soon as Buster settled down with his book his sister appeared. She was dressed up for a date – except for her hair which was in its usual tangle.

"You look great," said Buster, before she could speak. "I swear I haven't touched your hairbrush. It was probably little brother Zack this time. You can borrow mine if you like." He put the brush in her hand and kissed her cheek.

Wide-eyed, his sister backed out of the room.

Buster's father got home late that night, and straight after dinner he made a beeline for Buster. "Now about these test results ... "

"I can see it's worrying for you," said Buster.

His father's jaw dropped. "You can?"

"Well, naturally. Why don't we go into your study and talk it over."

Buster's mother said, "Oh stop picking on the poor boy all the time. You never give him a chance.

Before his father could reply, Buster said, "Sorry, Mum,

this is a private fight. You and I can have a chat later. Coming, Dad?"

Open-mouthed, his father followed him.

As they went into the study Buster said, "As I was saying, the problem is there just isn't enough time for all-round sport and study, something's got to give. If you want better test results I'll have to give something up."

"Not the football," said his father determinedly. "I want you in that team. Family tradition."

"Couldn't agree more," said Buster. "But I'm afraid if you want better results in my school tests some of the other stuff's got to go ... The track and field maybe. I'm sure we can sort it out ... " And so they did.

Chapter 10

Bill

The friends did all the usual things that weekend. Everything was the same – yet everything was different.

Kim went shopping with her mother. She hated it as usual, but it didn't matter too much. She knew that as soon as she was back in her room she would be enjoying the torments of Cathy's doomed love for Heathcliff.

Sam went for a drive in the country with his parents. His body was in the back of the family car but his mind was on the run in war-torn Europe, looking for the secret of *Greenmantle*.

Arnie went for a nice walk with his parents – but as they strolled through the neatly laid-out park he was fleeing through the wild heather with Alan Breck.

Amy baby-sat for her mother on Saturday night – and went down the aisle on the arm of her soldier lover. It was a wonderful wedding.

Buster did some revision and worked out with his father in their home gym – when he wasn't chasing cattle rustlers down the Chisum Trail ...

Willy mooched around at a loose end. He did all his homework, and he tidied his room till it could be tidied no more. He did his share of household jobs and he took baths and showers until his skin shone, killing off all known germs. Willy worked through all his favourite worries from the ozone layer to Earth being struck by a meteorite – and found that they were beginning to bore him.

There seemed to be something missing in his life. Surely it couldn't be mystery, adventure, excitement? The clash of swords, the clinking of tankards, the laughter of friends? The thrill of taking a risk for the sheer hell of it? Not worrying about a thing?

That sort of behaviour just wasn't sensible. The world was a dangerous place. It was his duty to worry ...

It all came to a head at school at break-time the next Monday. Even in a school that's all computers and high technology some things don't change. Break-time is one of them. Kids released from school for fifteen minutes, running, jumping, playing games, eating, chatting, strolling around. Fifteen precious minutes of freedom.

Another thing that doesn't change is the school bully. At this school it was a character called Clagger – very large, very dim, and very nasty. Always on the verge of being expelled, always being given another chance.

Progressive-minded teachers were always hoping to use reason and kindness to appeal to Clagger's better nature. It was a mistake – Clagger didn't have one. He wasn't really a bully in the worst sense, more of a petty nuisance really – a permanent pain in the neck.

When Willy mooched into the playground and saw Clagger slouching towards him, he knew he was in for something. A kick, a tweak, a punch, a trip – something.

Willy was one of Clagger's favourite victims.

He tried to pass Clagger without catching his eye or attracting his attention. For a moment he thought he had made it. Then, just as they passed each other, Clagger's long, ape-like arm shot out and his finger and thumb delivered a savage flick to one of Willy's bat-wing ears.

It hurt. There was a time when Willy would have taken it and moved on, thankful to have got off so lightly. But not this time. This wasn't quite the same Willy.

He heard a voice in his ear saying, "Nothing frightens Veelee!" Willy spun round and hurled himself on Clagger. Such was the force of the attack that the astonished

Clagger was knocked right off his feet.

Willy, who didn't have the slightest idea about fighting, didn't know what to do next. He clung on to Clagger like a large but feeble spider thinking, "As soon as he gets up he'll murder me." Which was exactly what would have happened – but this was Willy's lucky day. Arnie came out into the playground, saw what was happening, and rushed up to tell Sam, Kim and Amy who were on the far side of the big playground.

"Willy's gone mad and set about Clagger. He'll be murdered."

Arnie dashed off to the rescue and Kim turned to Amy. "Go and get Buster, right away. Come on, Sam."

Arnie returned to the scene of the trouble just as Clagger shook off Willy, lumbered to his feet and prepared to flatten his attacker. Arnie launched himself like a guided missile, and Clagger was knocked off his feet once again.

Clagger shrugged him off and started to get up again – only to be hit by a thin, bony missile called Kim and a very solid one called Sam. He went down yet again under their combined weights, and began flailing about wildly. Winded but game, Willy hurled himself back into the struggle. Arnie jumped on top of the lot of them.

The pile of bodies heaved and writhed for quite a while. Then Clagger shook off his attackers and staggered to his feet, like Gulliver fighting off the pygmies of Lilliput. He was deciding which of his many attackers to destroy first when a massive hand fell on his shoulder. Buster had arrived.

Buster was just as big as Clagger. He was fitter, and stronger too.

"Having a bit of trouble, Claggie?" said Buster amiably.

"All these kids jumped on me. I'll murder them."

"Bit of a problem there," said Buster. "All these kids happen to be mates of mine. I'd take it very personally if you murdered them." He tightened his grip on Clagger's shoulder. "Let's get you cleaned up a bit, shall we? See if we can work out a peaceful settlement. One that doesn't necessarily involve me beating you to a pulp. I hate violence … "

Winking at the others, Buster led the bemused Clagger away.

Kim looked at Willy. "What happened? Who started it?"

"He did," said Willy. "He spanged my ear so I jumped him."

"Well, it's a good job we turned up," said Sam.

"Lucky I found Buster so quickly," said Amy.

"I know," said Willy simply. He looked around the little group of his friends. "All for one, and one for all!"

Arnie gave him a baffled look. "Come again, Willy?"

"Never mind," said Willy, "Oh, and please don't call me Willy any more. From now on the name's Bill."

An excited junior rushed up. "You're to report to the Headmaster at once, Willy. He saw the whole thing on the playground surveillance camera. You're in trouble now."

"I'm not worried," said the brave new Bill. And he really wasn't.

He got off lightly in his interview with the Head. Thanks to his previous good record he escaped with a mild ticking off.

"I used to be afraid that you were too good to be true," said the Headmaster. "I'm rather relieved to discover you're not! Just behave yourself in future Willy, and we'll let this go."

"I'll try, sir – as long as no one picks on me. By the way, sir, it's not Willy – it's Bill."

Willy, or rather Bill, went back to the Library that very evening. Alone and unafraid he crossed the bridge, went through the twisted streets of Old Town and climbed the hill to the Library. He pushed open the big metal door and went inside. He crossed the vast lobby, lit by shafts of light from the stained-glass windows and went up to the gleaming wooden counter where the Guardian stood waiting.

She looked down at him. "It's Willy, isn't it?" She looked harder. "No, I'm sorry. Now I look closer, I can see it's Bill."

"That book I looked at yesterday ... "

The Guardian reached under the counter and produced a leather-bound volume. "*Tales of the Musketeers*? I've got it here for you. I hoped you'd be back."

She opened the book to a coloured illustration in the front. It showed five musketeers in a tavern, each with sword in one hand, tankard in the other. They were drinking a toast.

"This picture is a bit of a puzzle," said the Guardian. "I can recognise D'Artagnan, Athos, Porthos and Aramis but who's the fifth musketeer?"

Willy grinned. "The tall, thin one with the ears, you mean? He's called Veelee!"

The Guardian stamped the book and Bill took it away.

As she watched him go the Guardian thought, "Well, maybe you *can* win 'em all – sometimes."

The door slammed behind him and she went back to her lonely vigil with the books – waiting for people to come and find the magic.

Bill walked down the hill, carried on through Old Town, and stopped at the little café.

"Evening, Bill," said the café man. "Care for some lemonade?" He sat down at an outside table, took a swig of lemonade and opened the book …

… and found himself at a corner table in a crowded, smoky tavern. D'Artagnan, Athos, Porthos and Aramis were with him and he was showing them a plan. "All we have to do is avoid the Cardinal's Guards, climb over the palace roof, get in the attic window, make our way to the Cardinal's bedchamber, open his secret safe and recover the Queen's necklace."

"Rob the Cardinal's palace?" said Athos.

"Of course, it's certain death if we're caught," said Porthos.

"Which we certainly will be!" said Aramis.

"If Veelee says it can be done, then we'll do it!" said D'Artagnan.

"That's the idea," said Bill. "All for one – and one for all!"